Bright Summaries.com

A bottle in the Gaza Sea

BY VALÉRIE ZENATTI

Written by Lucile Lhoste
Translated by Oliver Brown

A bottle in the Gaza Sea

by VALÉRIE ZENATTI

BOOK ANALYSIS
BOOK ANALYSIS
Bright Summaries.com
Little Fires Everywhere
BY CELESTE NG

VALÉRIE ZENATTI

FRENCH AUTHOR, TRANSLATOR AND SCREENWRITER

- **Born in 1970 in Nice**

- **Some of his works:**

  - *When I was a soldier* (2002), autobiography

  - *Late for war* (2006), novel

  - *Jacob, Jacob* (2014), novel

Valérie Zenatti was born in Nice on 1 April 1970. At the age of 13, she emigrated with her family to Israel, where she did her military service between 1988 and ˉ990. She then returned to France where she studied history and Hebrew. As a translator for the Israeli writer Aharon Appelfeld (born in 1932), she worked in a variety of jobs (in journalism, radio, and teaching) before devoting herself to writing novels and screenplays.

Her texts have won her various awards (including the Prix du Livre Inter for *Jacob, Jacob* in 2015), and two of her novels, *Une bouteille dans la mer de Gaza* and *En retard pour la guerre*, have been adapted into films.

A BOTTLE IN THE GAZA SEA

A HYMN TO INTERCULTURAL DIALOGUE

- **Genre:** children's novels

- **Reference edition:** *Une bouteille dans la mer de Gaza*, Paris, L'École des loisirs, coll. « Médium », 2005

- **1st edition:** 2005

- **Themes:** Israeli-Palestinian conflict, war, friendship, dialogue

In the aftermath of a terrorist attack near her home, 17-year-old Tal has a crazy idea: write a letter of friendship and hope, seal it in a bottle and ask her brother Eytan to take it with him to Gaza and put it in the sea. The schoolgirl hopes that the bottle will be found by a teenager her own age with whom she can correspond. Unexpectedly, it is a young man who answers her, and he does not seem very friendly…

Translated into some fifteen languages and awarded several prizes, *A Bottle in the Gaza Sea* was also adopted for the cinema by Thierry Binisti (French director, born in 1964) in 2012.

SUMMARY

FORCING A DIALOGUE

Tal, a young Israeli teenager, lives with her parents and brother in Jerusalem, where war has become part of her daily life. For three years and the beginning of the second Intifada (nationalist revolt of the Palestinians), there has been one attack after another. One of them, which occurred in a café near her home, shocked the high school student who is not used to so much violence. She loves her city, her daily life, and her friends and can no longer stand so much instability and conflict between Israelis and Palestinians.

 ## DID YOU KNOW THAT?

The first Intifada took place between 1987 and 1993 in the West Bank and Gaza, Palestinian territories occupied by Israel. Exasperated by the daily humiliations they suffered and indignant at the minimisation of the death of four Palestinians in an accident caused by an Israeli truck, the Palestinians, mainly young people, began a campaign of civil disobedience accompanied by acts of violence (stone-throwing, Molotov cocktail attacks, etc.). This campaign ended with the 1993 Oslo

Accords, which established a progressive autonomy plan for the occupied territories. However, these agreements were a failure.

While she usually writes down her memories and emotions for herself, one day, had as an epiphany: she needs to get in touch with someone on the other side of the border with Gaza. She decides to write a long letter, which she places in a bottle and gives to her brother Eytan, who is doing his military service in the Palestinian city. She asks him to throw the bottle into the sea and hopes that someone will find it and agree to talk to her.

Sometime later, an e-mail arrives at the address Tal created especially for this exchange. To her surprise, it came from a man who refused to play along. However, the young Israeli manages to force a dialogue and begins an ongoing correspondence with the man who calls himself Gazaman.

A few months later, while Tal is walking around Jerusalem to film the city for a documentary, an attack occurs before her eyes. This event upsets her life, makes her more serious and bitter, and leads her to push her pen pal to the limit. The latter ends up confessing his first name, Naïm, and shares with her the way he lives his daily life and the war in the Gaza Strip.

Six months after finding the bottle, Naim writes Tal what will be his last message. He details everything she wanted to know about him, tells her about his recent admission to a scholarship in Canada, and arranges to meet her three years later at the Trevi Fountain in Rome.

A SECRET CORRESPONDENCE

Relations between Israelis and Palestinians are not well thought of, which is why Eytan is initially shocked by his sister's request: isn't she crazy to want to talk to a Palestinian in a time of war? Moreover, carrying such a message puts him in danger himself, for the same reasons. Nevertheless, he finally gives in, out of consideration for his little sister.

Tal has created a new e-mail address, especially for this correspondence, which she checks frequently for the next two weeks, at the end of which she receives a message from a certain Gazaman. He immediately shatters the girl's beautiful illusions: she is lucky that her bottle was found by someone who knows Hebrew because hardly anyone in Gaza speaks the language, and he has no desire to respond to her requests...

However, these statements are not as true as the author would have us believe. He is basically very intrigued by Tal and her sincerity, and can't help going to the Internet café to answer her, being careful not to let anyone catch him. It is indeed dangerous to have cordial contact with an Israeli in Gaza. One day, thinking that he has been found out and fearing the consequences, he decides to stop going to the cybercafé and to use a computer in a room run by friends in order to keep in touch with the girl.

However, he remains very suspicious for several months, refusing to reveal anything concrete about him. Tal only learns about it much later, but Eytan knows a minimum about Naïm. The soldier regularly watched the Gaza beach where he dropped the bottle out of curiosity and caught the moment when the Palestinian found the letter. He knew from the beginning what the young man looked like, but preferred to keep this detail to himself, although he admits that he trusted him from the start.

A FRIENDSHIP ACROSS BORDERS

For a long time, Naïm remains completely silent about his life and his past. It is only at the end of the novel when he is about to leave for Canada, that he reveals to her that he was working for his scholarship. The reader also learns that Tal reminds him of another girl with the same name, whom he knew in Israel when he worked there. He stayed with his father, also his employer, and gradually fell in love with the other Tal. After the outbreak of the second Intifada in 2000, young Palestinians like him could no longer work in Israel. So Naim vowed to leave Gaza to build a better future elsewhere.

During their exchanges, Tal receives a proposal from her father that interests her in particular: to make a documentary on Jerusalem by filming the city as she sees it. One morning, she witnesses the explosion of a bus in the middle of the street, while several people were on board. After that, she did not answer Naïm for several days. Tal was already worried about what was going on around her, but after the bus bombing, she barely left her house, had to see a psychologist and was completely distraught.

Gradually, her correspondence with Naïm becomes a refuge: she talks to him more easily than to the practitioner, to whom she agrees to confide only after several sessions. Her father nevertheless manages to shake her out of her lethargy by taking her for a walk in town. This is necessary for her to confess all about her correspondence, which he accepts without flinching. Tal then has a bad feeling, as Naïm has not sent her a message for a while. This is confirmed by the separation that occurs when he announces his intention to leave the country, despite the promise of a meeting three years later.

CHARACTER STUDY

TAL LEVINE

Tal is a 17-year-old high school student, born on July 1, 1986 in Tel Aviv – while all her family members were born in Jerusalem for several generations. According to Naïm, who discovers her at the same time as the reader when she sends him her photo by e-mail, she has an angular, open face, long chestnut hair, brown-green eyes and freckles. She is pretty without being extremely beautiful. She is easy to talk to and has a cheerful disposition, although she is very concerned about the war situation in her country.

Her environment and quality of life are quite comfortable despite the latent insecurity. The teenager knows, however, that it is difficult to talk about dialogue with the Palestinians, which is why she does not talk about her correspondence with Naim until very late. When they find out, her parents are surprisingly tolerant: deep down, they are not closed to an agreement either, even if they cannot express it openly because of the tensions between the two territories.

Her main relationships are with Efrat, her best friend, Heri, her boyfriend, and his sister, with whom she also gets along well. She is also very close to her brother Eytan, a 20-year-old military nurse, with whom she often goes to the same café when he is on leave. This is one of the reasons why the attack at the beginning of the novel in the café in question affects her so much: it is a place that is familiar to her.

Tal has lived through important events in Israeli history, two of which have had a particular impact on her: the signing of the Oslo Accords in 1993 (a step in the Israeli-Palestinian peace process that put an end to the first Intifada) and the assassination of Yitzhak Rabin (Israeli politician, 1922-1995). Every year, she and her family go to the place where he was killed to commemorate this fateful date.

 ## YITZHAK RABIN

Born in Israel into a Zionist family, Yitzhak Rabin joined the Jewish underground army after school, fighting for the independence of the country then under British mandate. He rose through the ranks, becoming Chief of Staff of Tsahal (the name given to the Israeli army at the time of independence in 1948) in 1964, before becoming ambassador to Washington for five years.

In 1974, he entered politics as Minister of Labour before becoming, the same year, Prime Minister following Golda Meir (1898-1978). He became Minister of Defence and was inflexible in the face of the Palestinian uprising of 1987. Later, during a second term as Prime Minister in 1992, he reversed his position and began to work for peace between Israelis and Palestinians, to the point of receiving the Nobel Peace Prize in 1994. Unfortunately, his efforts did not make him happy and, the following year, during a demonstration in support of the government, he was assassinated by an ultra-nationalist fanatic.

Like many Israelis, Tal lives with the regular attacks in the country. However, she does not get used to so much violence and conflict. Her desire to live one day in a peaceful land where Israelis and Palestinians can live together is the driving force behind her decision to throw a bottle into the Gaza Sea.

The bus explosion she witnesses shakes her to the point that she no longer goes to school, but she cannot help but keep an unshakeable faith that her dream of reconciliation will come true. However, she does not take any great action in this direction, her correspondence with a Palestinian being her only form of resistance to the barbarity. But in doing so, she is already taking a major risk and showing exceptional courage for her age.

If she hopes to converse with another girl about her concerns, she is doubly surprised by the effect of her bottle. Not only does a man find her, but he also shows her through his testimony that Palestinian youth is even more distressed than she thought. Tal understands that there is suffering on both sides and that the Palestinians, presented as enemies, are also suffering the heavy consequences of the war. As a teenager, she remains powerless in the face of the conflict, but she finds a way to cross the border into the Gaza Strip and establish a dialogue.

NAÏM AL-FARJOUK

Naïm is 20 years old at the time of the story and was probably born around 1983 or 1984, according to the years during which he corresponds with Tal. He is quite tall and has short, curly hair. He has a teasing temperament and is much less naive and playful than his pen pal. He is an only child – a rarity in Gaza – and is pampered by his parents.

Unlike most Palestinians, Naim knows Hebrew because his father insisted that he learn it when the Israeli-Palestinian peace process began. He is very good academically and works hard to make a better life for himself, managing to get a scholarship to Canada. His social life is poor apart from his two European friends, Paolo and Willy, psychologists, whose computer he borrows after deciding to stop going to the Internet café.

When he was about the same age as Tal, he had the opportunity to work in Israel. He had to stay there after the checkpoints to Gaza were blocked and then regularly came to his boss's house to eat and/or sleep. It was there that he met another Tal, his employer's daughter, and fell in love with her. Unfortunately, he had to return to Gaza soon after because there was no more work for him, and he could not go back because of the increasing number of attacks on Israeli soil. This brutal break deeply marked him: he no longer wants to be in a place where his relationships are conditioned by the slightest act of violence.

Naïm is very suspicious and reluctant to reveal himself. Even with his friends, it takes him a long time to confide in them. Paolo and Willy's words about the possibility for an individual to exist within himself, to be able to heal his tears, are what upset him and push him to finally open up. The two psychologists are in fact in Palestine because, if we cannot prevent conflicts, we can on the other hand support those who suffer them to help them heal their wounds. Listening to them, and considering them as individuals instead of an anonymous part of a collective, is for them the basis of their work. Naïm, who has suffered a lot, breaks down when he hears these words.

In his correspondence with Tal, he initially uses the nickname Gazaman, only gives his first name in a period of great fatigue following actions affecting acquaintances, and only really speaks of himself in his final message, when he is certain that the girl will no longer have the opportunity to reply.

By the time the story begins, he has been through a lot. His initial reluctance to continue their exchange, however, has little to do with the conflict; it is mainly due to the memory of the other Tal that still haunts him. He gradually understands that just because his pen pal is young doesn't necessarily mean she is brainless, and he begins to hope that it is still possible, so long after his confinement in Gaza, to form a real relationship with the Other. With this in mind, and relieved to know that someone is waiting for him at the end of the road, he can confidently leave to continue his studies abroad.

EYTAN LEVINE

Eytan is a 20-year-old military nurse and Tal's older brother. Like all young Israelis of his age, he is obliged to do his military service as the law requires that every young man or woman, except in exceptional family situations (if the young person has children for example), completes up to three years in the army. He serves in the Gaza Strip but doesn't talk much about his life there. Tal assumes that he hides the horrors he witnesses from her so as not to traumatise her: "I imagine he has learned not to see, or to forget, so as not to look too much like an old man." (p. 9)

Naturally calm and composed, he is already a very mature young man, who is fully aware of the seriousness of the Israeli-Palestinian conflict. He seems quite open, even if he is less so than his sister: unlike her, he is not overly optimistic about the possibility of a friendship between the two sides. Even though he agrees, albeit reluctantly, to deliver Tal's message to Gaza, he takes precautions: he checks the contents of the letters first, and only acts when he is sure that he cannot be seen (his behaviour might be considered suspicious), and then returns several times, always checking his back, in the hope of seeing the person picking up the bottle.

However, these details are only revealed at the end of the novel, when Eytan reveals his secret: he is the only one who knows what Naïm looks like since he saw him take the letter. It is on this same occasion that he loses his temper with his sister, which is very rare and highlights the distance that separates them: "I mean, do you live on Mars or what? Did you really think I was going to throw a bottle into the sea, in Gaza, without knowing anything about its content? I'm a soldier, Tal. Not a sweet, irresponsible dreamer" (p. 143).

OURI AND EFRAT

Ouri and Efrat are two Israeli teenagers, Tal's boyfriend and best friend respectively. They go to the same high school as her, but only Efrat is in the same class as her friend (they make sure they are next to each other in class). They are only indirectly confronted with the conflict, so they find it difficult to console Tal when she witnesses the bus attack. However, they are very considerate towards her, and one can even say that their state of mind is changing more remarkably since this act of violence has directly affected their friend.

While Efrat is only sporadically mentioned in the rest of the plot, Tal frequently questions her feelings about Ouri. She tells her father that she still loves the boy, or so she thinks but admits that she would choose Naim if there was a choice to be made.

TAL'S PARENTS

Tal and Eytan's parents are the only Israeli characters (along with the other Tal's family, but the latter's feelings are not particularly detailed) who experienced the beginning of the peace process and understood its ins and outs. Tired of the conflicts between Israel and Palestine, they had high hopes for the 1993 Oslo Accords, which were supposed to bring the two countries together. Tal makes this clear when she recounts the day of 13 September 1993 in the Levines' home: they did not go to work, bought unusual food and drink, and cried with joy at the television showing the Israeli, Palestinian and American leaders together.

They have since become disillusioned and lead, like any Israeli, a day-to-day life, without knowing where the conflict will lead the next day. However, they have not abandoned their pacifist ideas and keep faith in the dialogue that they believe is still possible between the two communities. This is why, without showing the same overflowing enthusiasm as their daughter (no doubt they are morally tired of this conflict), they encourage her in the trust she places in Naïm.

KEYS TO READING

THE ISRAELI-PALESTINIAN CONFLICT

This geopolitical conflict has its origins in the Balfour Declaration (named after its signatory, the British Secretary of State Arthur Balfour, 1848-1930) in 1917. In this document, the United Kingdom declared itself in favour of a Jewish national home in Palestine, while the Arabs expected the creation of an independent Arab state promised by the Hussein-McMahon Agreement two years earlier.

Following the Second World War (1939-1945), the British, unable to find a satisfactory solution to reconcile the Jewish and Palestinian points of view and to stop the violence, handed over their mandate over this territory to the UN, which voted in November 1947 for a partition plan of Palestine dividing it into three parts: a Jewish state, an Arab state and an international zone (Jerusalem). This resolution, rejected by the Palestinians, triggered a real civil war. When, in May of the following year, Israel declared its independence, the war was official and inaugurated the warlike period that this region of the world is still experiencing today.

The disagreement is mainly based on the lack of mutual recognition of the two peoples and the non-recognition of the existence of a Palestinian state by some UN members. In addition to this confrontation over territory, the two entities are also opposed from a religious point of view: Palestine is predominantly Muslim while Israel is Zionist (imbued with a strong Jewish national sentiment).

Prior to the events of the Palestinian uprising in 2000 mentioned by Tal and Naïm, various solutions were envisaged to end the conflict. The Camp David Accords, signed in 1978 by Egyptian President Anwar Sadat (1918-1981) and Israeli Prime Minister Menachem Begin (1913-1992), provided, among other things, a basis for negotiating the fate of the Gaza Strip. The Oslo Accords, signed in 1993 in the presence of Yitzhak Rabin, Yasser Arafat (Palestinian statesman, 1929-2004) and Bill Clinton (US President, born 1946), planned a gradual autonomy for Palestine, establishing a national authority and a clear division of the territories. Their implementation was slowed down by the assassination of Rabin in 1995 and then abandoned after the start of the second Intifada.

This conflict is currently unresolved and further strained by the fact that, since the 2014 Gaza war and the resulting wave of violence from 2015 onwards, relations between Israel and Palestine have worsened further.

THE MODE OF CORRESPONDENCE

The novel has several different types of narration: it constantly alternates between chapters with classical narration, presented sometimes by Tal and sometimes by Naïm, and chapters with e-mails between the two protagonists.

In the chapters where they speak for themselves, they give free rein to their concerns and feelings. They ask questions they cannot share with others and make observations that form the basis for their unusual relationship.

> *"I told him that the questions wouldn't arise if I wasn't Israeli and he wasn't Palestinian. But that's the way it is: we were born where the land burns, where young people feel old very early, where it's almost a miracle when someone dies a natural death." (p. 69)*

In their e-mails, on the other hand, since they are likely to be read by a third party, Tal and Naïm reveal little, often preferring to talk about lighter subjects. These e-mails are presented with their addressees, recipients and objects, and the tone is often freer than in the classic chapters, even though they are narrated by the same characters.

> *"Special features: claims to be polite but writes "Hi, Machine". Has a sense of humour, I would say Jewish humour. A taste for secrecy, too." (p. 51)*

Much later, and in only one instance, do Tal and Naim talk via instant messaging. During this conversation, Naïm makes the bitter observation that Israelis and Palestinians have never agreed on the words they use and that this fact alone constitutes an obstacle to their understanding. This reflection arises from the fact that they are now aware that they do not use the same terms to designate the same things:

"You say that you are looking for terrorists in the city of Shechem and we say that you are looking for our fighters in the city of Nablus. (And it's the same city! And they are the same men!)" (p. 139)

The choice of correspondence as a mode of narration follows a rational logic: since the story must remain within a realistic framework, it was impossible for the author to send Tal to Palestine (she is not yet old enough to do her military service like Eytan). The only way she can start a dialogue with the other side is by sending a message; in this case in the form of letters and then e-mails. This stylistic choice has a practical reason above all.

However, one can also recognise, in the political statements of the protagonists, a denunciation of a current situation, as other epistolary novels have done. This tradition is far from new: in 1721, in *The Persian Letters*, Montesquieu (French writer and thinker, 1689-1755) was already criticising the French society of his time, but in a more roundabout way to get around the censorship. Here, the aim is to make teenagers on the verge of becoming world citizens admit the absurdity of the conflict, by giving a voice directly to two of them.

THE HOPES OF THE YOUTH OF THE MIDDLE EAST

The two protagonists are representatives of a youth who took hope in a reconciliation between Israel and Palestine when the first peace agreements they knew (the Oslo agreements) were signed, and who do not understand how the situation can degenerate like this when both peoples claim to want the conflict to subside: "One day you, we, will realise that there is no possible winner in the violence, that it is a war of losers. A mess." (p. 166)

While they continue to hope for a happy outcome, following the failure of the Oslo Accords, they have become fatalistic: nothing seems to be getting better at home and they no longer know what they can do to try to improve the situation. As the violence continues, the population seems to have come to terms with – or rather resigned to – the fact that the conflict continues. Tal explains that, after the café attack and then the bus attack, life seems to go on because, given the frequency of the attacks, it is obvious to everyone that one can only live hoping not to be among the future victims.

On the side of Naim, it is more complicated. The people live relatively normally, except for the military presence, but are both cut off from the world and stigmatised to the extreme by their Jewish neighbours. They live from day to day, waiting to be recognised as a state, distrustful of each other (Naim is careful not to show the slightest sympathy towards the Israelis in public) and eager to regain their freedom.

Since the autumn of 2015, as a result of the Knife Intifada, many media outlets have taken stock of the motivations that drive young Palestinians to revolt both against Israel and against all authority. As they have noted, they are "for the most part born after the Oslo agreements, have grown up with the now proven failure of the 'peace process', in permanent frustration, fear and humiliation, with no prospect of a future" (WARSCHAWSKI M., "La jeunesse palestinienne à couteaux tirés avec Israël", in *Association France Palestine Solidarité*, October 2015). These young people only know their land, and what they have learned from the Arab Spring (a series of uprisings that took place in Arab countries from 2011 onwards) has accentuated their feeling of injustice regarding their own situation. She is desperate, no longer hesitating to take up arms because she has seen one attempt at a diplomatic resolution of the conflict after another fail.

Tal and Naim also see no solution, but unlike most Jews and Palestinians past and present, they refuse to see violence as having any positive effect; they prefer dialogue to arms because they have both witnessed the shattering consequences of war.

SOME QUESTIONS TO HELP YOU THINK MORE DEEPLY...

- "These are days of darkness, sadness and horror. Fear has returned." (p. 7) In what way do these opening sentences summarise the heroine's state of mind at the time? How will it change? Answer with evidence from the novel.

- The plot takes place between September 2003 and mid-2004, when the second Intifada has been raging for three years. What impact does this context of war have on the Israeli and Palestinian populations? Answer by quoting elements of the correspondence between Tal and Naim.

- The historical-political context plays an important role in the novel. How is it essential for understanding the psychology of the characters?

- Why do Tal and Naim have to hide their correspondence, and why does it seem absurd to do so?

- Is the reaction of Tal's family when they learn of her email exchange with a Palestinian surprising? Justify your answer.

- Eytan's military status is reminiscent of the service that all young Israeli men and women must perform in the army. Despite this status, is Eytan in the same frame of mind as his sister or does he see the conflict differently?

- The end of the novel is open-ended, whereas the director of the film has chosen to imagine the future meeting of the two young people. In your opinion, what is the interest of these two orientations?

- How would you transcribe the epistolary exchanges between the two protagonists onto the screen? Why would you do this?

- How does this quote from Naim echo the desperation of Palestinian youth?

> *"I must be the only Palestinian in Gaza for whom someone on the other side cares. Unesco should designate me as a historical monument or world heritage. I should be filmed and shown to the world, like a rare and precious object." (p. 85)*

- Do the characters of Tal and Naim reflect today's youth in Israel and Palestine? What makes them different?

TO GO FURTHER

REFERENCE EDITION

ZENATTI V., *Une bouteille dans la mer de Gaza*, Paris, L'École des loisirs, coll. « Médium », 2005, 167 p.

BASELINE STUDY

WARSCHAWSKI M., « La jeunesse palestinienne à couteaux tirés avec Israël », in *Association France Palestine Solidarité*, October 2015, accessed on 27 September 2016. http://www.france-palestine.org/La-jeunesse-palestinienne-a-couteaux-tires-avec-Israel

FILM ADAPTATION

Une bouteille à la mer, film directed by Thierry Binisti, with Agathe Bonitzer (Tal) and Mahmoud Shalaby (Naïm), France, Quebec, Israel, 2012.

The film's plot is quite similar to that of Valérie Zenatti's novel, with a voice-over reading the emails. However, the events take place over a year (as opposed to half the time in the book), some secondary characters are erased, Naïm studies at the French Cultural Centre in Gaza instead of going to Canada, and the plot goes a bit further than the end of the novel by imagining Tal and Naïm meeting. This film received several awards between 2011 and 2012.

Your opinion is important to us!
Leave a comment on the website of your online bookshop
and share your favourites on social networks!